Oliver and the BIG green snake

Jan Godfrey

Illustrated by Philip Norman

Scripture Union
130 City Road London EC1V 2NJ

© Jan Godfrey 1995

First published 1995

ISBN 0 86201 966 4

British Library Cataloguing-in-Publication Data.
A catalogue record for this book is available from the British Library.

Printed and bound in Great Britain by Cox and Wyman Ltd, Reading.

Contents

For Edward

Oliver and the snowflakes

Oliver was four, getting on for five. He had fair hair and bright blue eyes and he lived at number seven, The Crescent with his mum and dad, the twin babies Sam and Charlotte, and Zippy the tabby cat.

One winter morning Oliver woke up and saw straight-away that his bedroom looked different. The daylight was brighter than usual.

'Look!' said Mum, drawing back the curtains to let in the morning, 'It's snowing!'

Oliver looked, and could see soft white flakes pouring out of the sky.

'The garden's all white,' said Oliver, 'and the window's got a pattern on it like feathers!'

He could hardly wait to go out and play in the snow. Dad swept the path and trudged off to work while Mum bathed the twins and washed up. Oliver hoped that Mum might have time to take him out with his sledge.

She kept an eye on Oliver from the kitchen window. He ran about the garden and made lots of footprints and chased the snowflakes.

'There's millions of snowflakes!' said Oliver. 'Millions and zillions!'

Zippy the cat put a careful paw into the snow then rushed away indoors.

Everywhere felt very cold and quiet. The black branches of the trees were turning white, and there weren't any birds singing today. It was always quiet at the house next door, anyway, because nobody lived there. Mum had said there would be people in it one day very soon.

Oliver made a little snowman and he talked to it. He liked talking to things. Sometimes he talked to his little teddy bear Bruin.

'You're a very nice little snowman,' whispered Oliver.

'You're a very nice little boy,' the snowman whispered back.

Then all sorts of things happened. Oliver heard the sound of a big van pulling up in the snowy road at the front of the house. He could hear voices and shouting and barking, getting closer.

After a few minutes Oliver looked up from his snowman and saw two children and a huge dog peering over the fence at him through the snow. He saw a girl with lots of bright ginger curls, and a boy with a brown face and a big smile.

'Hallo!' said the boy. 'My name's Vimal. We're Moving In. I'm five.'

Oliver wasn't sure what Moving In meant, so he stared.

'I'm Polly,' said the girl. 'I'm six. We're going to live here with our special mum and dad. Our dog's called Honey. I saw you talking to your snowman. What's your name?'

'Oliver,' said Oliver. He felt shy. He gathered up his

little snowman awkwardly and ran into the kitchen. Mum was upstairs now.

'Is that you, Oliver?' called Mum.

Oliver didn't answer. He was looking round the kitchen. He'd just thought of a *very* good hidey-hole for his snowman.

'Come on, snowman,' said Oliver. 'You're going to hide in the food cupboard. You can eat a biscuit if you're hungry.'

He reached up and carefully opened the door. He pushed the snowman in beside the cereal boxes and tins and jars and packets. But the snowman started to break into cold squashy pieces so Oliver slammed the door shut quickly and went back into the garden. The next-door children had vanished from the fence and Oliver could hear them playing somewhere in their new garden.

After a few minutes Mum joined him. 'There's our new neighbours moving in,' said Mum. 'We'll ask them in to have some soup with us later. I'll make a big treacle tart.'

Soon Mum was chatting to Polly and Vimal's mum and dad over the fence. Oliver scowled. He didn't want all these strangers in his kitchen.

Vimal and Polly left Honey safely behind and came into Oliver's garden out of the way of the removal men. Oliver still felt shy of his new neighbours. He watched them throw snowballs at each other. Then Polly said to Vimal: 'Let's make a snowman.'

Oliver suddenly remembered his little snowman and he rushed indoors, followed by Vimal and Polly. The cupboard was empty. Mum was mopping up a lot of water, surrounded by tins of soup and soggy packets of food. The twins were in their high chairs banging spoons and screaming.

'Where's my little snowman?' shouted Oliver. 'He talked to me and I hid him in the food cupboard to keep him safe.'

'Oh OLIVER,' said his mum, looking rather flustered. 'Snowmen like to be out in the snow, not in cupboards. Your snowman has melted all over everywhere. The flour and everything's all spoilt. There's no time now to make a big treacle tart – or get the sledge out.'

Mum sounded cross, and Oliver sucked his thumb. Then Polly took his hand, and Vimal said: 'Let's build that really big snowman together, Oliver.'

They looked at the melted snowman puddle again and they all began to giggle. They laughed and laughed. Even Mum laughed too and said: 'Whoever heard of a snowman in a food cupboard? I might have cooked him for lunch!'

Then everyone giggled again and the twins crowed loudly. Oliver began to feel much happier. Soon they were all having soup together.

In the afternoon it was still snowing. The children all went back outside and built a very large snowman together. Oliver forgot all about being shy with Vimal and Polly, and they told Oliver how they were looked after by a lovely special mum and dad called Sally and Dave because their own parents couldn't look after them any more.

Then a voice said: 'Hi!' and there was Oliver's dad home from work. 'I'm back early because of all the snow,' said Dad, pretending to shake hands with the snowman. 'I see we've got visitors.'

'They're my friends,' said Oliver proudly. 'They're Moving In.'

'Well now,' said Dad, 'perhaps we can help by Moving OUT – we'll go sledging in the park!'

Sledging together was great fun. By bedtime Oliver felt very sleepy.

Dad showed him a book with pictures of beautiful snowflakes.

'They're all different patterns,' said Oliver. 'But there's millions and zillions of snowflakes.'

'Just like us,' said Mum, tucking him up. 'God has made millions and zillions of people. All different, but we can all be friends.'

'I didn't like my friends at first,' said Oliver. 'They made me feel shy.'

'Perhaps *they* were shy of *you*,' suggested Mum.

'Oh,' said Oliver. He hadn't thought of that.

That night Oliver dreamt that white feathery snowflakes were drifting down into a thick, soft pillow. It was very cosy.

Before he fell asleep Oliver said to God: 'Thank you for making all those lovely different snowflakes. And thank you especially for my new friends. Amen. Goodnight.'

Oliver
and the chickenpoxes

Oliver felt very excited. That afternoon Mum was taking him next door to tea with Polly and Vimal, all on his own. He was looking forward to playing with their toys and trikes and cars. Sometimes Polly and Vimal's mum, Sally, took them to the park with Honey the dog, and gave them a lovely tea with things like fish fingers and baked beans and pink cakes and wobbly jelly.

At lunch-time the phone rang and Oliver's mum answered it.

'Oh, Oliver,' said Mum, putting down the receiver. 'I'm afraid you can't go next door to tea after all. Polly and Vimal have got chickenpox! They're both covered in spots and they don't feel well at all.'

Oliver was terribly, terribly disappointed. He felt angry and hot and cross inside, and he cried and he shouted and he shouted and he cried.

'I WANTED to go,' sobbed Oliver, stamping his feet. 'It's not FAIR. Stupid, silly old chickenpoxes.'

He grabbed his teddy bear Bruin. He put his thumb in his mouth and he stamped upstairs to his room. He slammed the door and tipped a box of toy cars on to the floor. Nobody cared that he was so disappointed. Nobody cared that he wanted to go to Polly and Vimal's house so badly.

'It's not FAIR,' said Oliver again. The tears rolled down his cheeks and he flung himself down on his bed.

Then Oliver had an idea. He stayed on his bed very still and quietly so that Mum would think he'd gone to sleep. Then he tiptoed to his box of crayons and felt-tipped pens. He chose a nice bright red felt pen, thick and chunky. Oliver knew this was naughty, but it was going to be fun.

'EVERYBODY'S going to have chickenpoxes,' said Oliver furiously. 'ALL the toys. I'm CROSS. Come on, Bruin, you're first.'

He pulled the top off the felt pen and made wet, splodgy, inky red spots all over Bruin. He thought he heard Bruin make a little grunting sound. He seemed to be saying that he did *not* want big red splodgy spots all over him, thank you, but Oliver didn't listen. He was being very, VERY naughty.

He put all his soft toys together in a long line on his bed and set to work with the red felt pen. It wasn't long before his patchwork giraffe and his stuffed monkey and a toy cat and a toy puppy and a rabbit and a panda and his lion pyjama case and lots of little teddy bears *all* had chickenpoxes. Oliver still felt hot and cross and disappointed and he *enjoyed* being naughty.

Then Oliver looked in the mirror and put inky red spots all over his own hot, red face. His reflection looked back at him, all hot and red and spotty too. He talked to his reflection in the mirror.

'Hallo, Oliver,' said the real Oliver to the mirror-Oliver. 'That was a good game, wasn't it? All the toys have got chickenpoxes now.'

He made his reflection say: 'Hallo, Oliver,' back at him in a funny squeaky-growly sort of voice. His throat felt a bit sore anyway, because he'd shouted and cried such a lot. He pulled a horrid face at the mirror-Oliver and put out his tongue, and the mirror-Oliver copied everything he did. But the mirror-Bruin didn't look very pleased.

Then Oliver heard Mum downstairs. She'd be coming up soon to find him.

Oliver quickly smeared his hands over his face, looking in the mirror to help him. But the spots all smudged together, except for one chickenpox that wouldn't go away. Suddenly he felt tired, and going out to tea didn't seem to matter quite so much. He hid the felt pen under his pillow and sat on the bed cuddling Bruin.

In came Mum. She had a yelling twin under each arm and she nearly tripped over one of the cars on the floor. She looked at the long line of spotty toys propped up on the bed all looking at her, and then she looked at Oliver's face. She was very angry.

'Oh OLIVER,' said Mum, 'whatever have you been doing? There's felt pen EVERYWHERE. You have been really, REALLY VERY NAUGHTY INDEED.'

Oliver cried. Mum didn't seem to understand that his toys had all got chickenpox spots too.

'It's a good thing it's washable ink,' said Mum. 'Bruin and those other poor toys will have to be scrubbed – *hard* – and so will you, Oliver.'

When Oliver's hands and face had been washed – *hard* – Mum looked at Oliver's smudgy red face again – and again, more closely.

'There was one chickenpox that wouldn't go away,' said Oliver.

'Oh OLIVER,' said Mum again. 'I think you've got more than one chickenpox – and it's not just an inky chickenpox either. You've got *real* chickenpox! Just like Polly and Vimal.'

'Oh,' said Oliver, 'I don't think I like having chickenpoxes. How will they go away if they don't wash off?'

'They'll go away when you start feeling better,' said Mum. 'God has made our bodies so that they can get well again after they've been ill.'

'Will the twins get chickenpoxes too?' asked Oliver. He wondered if Sam and Charlotte would have little chickenpoxes as they were only little babies.

'They might,' said Mum. 'And if they do I shall be very busy looking after you all.'

Oliver had to visit the doctor and go to bed. His legs ached and his head ached and he really didn't feel very well at all.

'I don't like being ill,' Oliver said to God. 'It's made me feel horrid and naughty. Please make me better, and Vimal and Polly too. Thank you.'

Mum looked after him with orange drinks and stories, and Dad cheered him up playing games and telling him more stories. He and Bruin were quite cosy, and Oliver even had a funny card from Dave and Sally next door telling him to get well soon. The card had a pop-out picture of a big spotty dog that opened its mouth and wagged its tail.

After a few days Oliver began to feel better. Mum helped him make a card for Polly and Vimal. Dad helped him draw a picture of Zippy the cat all spotty with chickenpoxes, and Oliver laughed and laughed and laughed.

'All that laughing will help make you better,'

said Dad.

'And my card will make Polly and Vimal better, too,' said Oliver.

Next day there was a surprise. There was a knock at the door and Oliver could hear Mum talking.

'How would you like to go to a chickenpox party soon at Polly's house?' called out Mum to Oliver. 'Some of the children from play-group and school are going – Scott and Vicky and Darren and Laura – they've all had chickenpox too!'

Oliver began to cheer up and look forward to the chickenpox party. It had almost been worth having chickenpoxes!

The party was tremendous fun. And this is what Oliver said to God before he went to sleep that night: 'Thank you, God, for making the chickenpoxes go away. Thank you for making me feel well again. Thank you for Mum and Dad and Vimal and Polly and Sally and Dave and all my friends. Amen. Goodnight.'

Oliver and the kite

It was a very windy day. The doors slammed, and the windows rattled, and everything clattered and banged. Honey barked and Zippy's fur blew the wrong way. The clouds scudded across the sky like a flock of white woolly sheep running very fast.

'What a blustery day!' said Oliver's mum, pegging out the washing. 'I hope it doesn't blow the twins' nappies off the line.'

On the washing line the clothes had filled out into funny fat shapes. Oliver's stripy pyjamas looked as if they had plump arms and legs. He imagined the wind had a big round face and puffy cheeks.

'I think the wind's wearing my pyjamas today,' said Oliver.

Sally and Dave next door took Oliver and Polly and Vimal and Honey up the hill to Top Common to fly Oliver's kite. The kite had a smiling face and a long string with beautiful blue streamers. Oliver liked his kite very much indeed. He showed it to Polly and Vimal.

'It's got a funny face,' said Vimal. 'It's smiling.'

'It's got lovely ribbons,' said Polly. 'It's pretty.'

'It should fly well,' said Dave. 'It's a super kite, Oliver.'

Vimal was allowed to hold Honey's lead as they reached Top Common. The wind blew harder than ever. Oliver held his kite tightly and hoped he wouldn't get knocked over by the strong gale. The trees at the edge of the common were swaying and rustling and Polly's curls kept blowing into her eyes.

As they all walked past the trees and bushes to reach the open part of the common, Honey began to get very excited. She went wild and started to chase all the leaves that were whirling about. She jumped up and down and barked and pulled at her lead. Suddenly she jerked the lead right out of Vimal's hand and dashed off in the opposite direction with the lead trailing behind her.

'Come back, Honey!' cried Vimal.

'Come back, at once, you naughty dog!' shouted Polly.

'Hold the kite safely, Oliver,' Sally called over her shoulder.

Oliver stood still. He thought he'd have a little chat to his kite while the others scrambled after Honey. They managed to catch hold of her and bring her back, and bent over her to fix her lead.

'Hallo, Kite,' said Oliver. 'It's very windy, isn't it?'

'Yes, yes, it is, it is,' said the kite excitedly, flapping up and down eagerly and smiling at Oliver. 'Are you going to fly me soon?'

'OK,' said Oliver, 'but your string's getting all tangled up.'

'Wheeeeeew!' whistled the wind, tugging at the kite. 'I want to play.'

20

'Don't interrupt,' said Oliver severely. 'You're very rude.'

'Hurry UP,' said the kite. 'Come ON.' And it *pulled* very hard.

Oliver held on as tightly as he could but the wind snatched at the kite. The string unravelled and the kite tried to fly away. But it didn't get very far. The wind caught it again and tossed it high up into one of the trees. It caught on the twigs and branches and flapped its face flat against the trunk.

'Stupid wind!' shouted Oliver. 'You've taken my kite away. Give me my kite back!'

He tried to pull at the string of the kite. But he reached too far. The others turned round in time to see Oliver falling over and disappearing head first into a big bush near the bottom of the tree.

'Ohhhh ...,' wailed Oliver. 'Ohhhh ...'

'Oh OLIVER,' said Vimal and Polly and Dave and Sally.

Oliver tried to scramble out of the bush which was leafy and prickly and full of twigs. But he couldn't move. His feet and his arms were firmly wedged. Whichever way he tried to turn there were branches in his way.

'I'm stuck,' wailed Oliver. 'Help me. I can't get out.'

'Don't worry,' said Dave, pushing the bush apart. 'Hang on in there and we'll soon rescue you.'

Vimal giggled and giggled and pulled at Oliver's legs, and Polly giggled and giggled and pulled at Oliver's arms.

Out came Oliver. He was covered from head to foot in twigs and leaves. His face and hands were very grubby. Sally dusted him down.

'My kite,' sobbed Oliver. 'I want my kite.'

'It's ever so high up in the tree,' said Vimal.

'It might be there for ever,' said Polly.

'We may not be able to get it down, Oliver,' said Sally gently.

Oliver cried and cried. By now a little crowd of people had gathered round the tree to see what was going on. They all looked at Oliver.

Then a man said: 'I think I can help. I live near here and I've got a ladder.'

The man was soon back with a long ladder. He put the ladder against the tree and looked up at the kite.

'It's very stuck, isn't it?' said Oliver with his thumb in his mouth.

'It's very stuck indeed,' said the man. 'But we'll have a go. I think I can rescue it and get it unstuck for you.'

The man climbed carefully up the ladder while everybody watched. He reached up – and up and at last the kite was free. Oliver was so happy when he saw its smiling face look down at him that he shouted: 'Hooray!!'

Everyone else said, 'Hooray!!' too, and Oliver said, 'Thank you,' lots of times to the man, when he'd climbed down again, for being so kind.

'I'll look out for your kite flying one day when it's been mended,' said the kind man to Oliver, and Oliver felt very pleased and proud.

The kite was a little bit torn in places. But it was still smiling.

Oliver held the kite very tightly all the way home. Near his house something stripy was blowing about in the air. It whirled about and then it landed on the fence.

'That's my pyjama top!' said Oliver. 'It's flying!'

'I think the wind's having a game with you today,'

23

said Dave, picking it up. 'And it's been stealing your mum's washing.'

Oliver's dad laughed and laughed when he heard everything that had been happening. He promised to mend the kite with some special glue.

Oliver's mum said: 'Oh OLIVER. What will you get up to next?' But she was pleased to see that the wind hadn't blown Oliver's pyjama top right away for ever.

At bedtime the wind had died down. Oliver said goodnight to his kite. It lay propped up against the chest of drawers beside teddy bear Bruin.

'Well, that was an adventure,' said the kite. 'We both got stuck. My face is a bit scratched. And my streamers aren't so good either.'

'My dad will mend you,' said Oliver. 'It was that silly old wind's fault. It was ever so strong. But I didn't see it, not ever.'

He thought about the invisible wind blowing trees and clouds and kites. He thought about his fat pyjamas billowing on the washing line, and that made him laugh. He began to feel sleepy. But before he fell asleep he said to God: 'I can't see you God, like I can't see that wind. But I'm glad you're always there.'

Oliver
and the chocolate mouse

It was nearly Dad's birthday, and Oliver wondered what to give him for a present.

'A hanky?' suggested Mum.

'No ...' said Oliver. 'He's got lots of hankies.'

'A pen?' suggested Mum again.

'No ...' said Oliver. 'Pens are boring.'

'A pair of socks?' suggested Mum once more.

'No ...' said Oliver. 'Socks are clothes, not presents.'

'Oh dear,' said Mum, 'you *are* hard to please, Oliver. We'll count the pennies in your money-box pig and go shopping tomorrow.'

Today was a play-group day. Oliver had a good time, painting and glueing a birthday card for Dad. He played with Amit and Charlie and Jennifer, and sat at their table when it was time for drinks and biscuits. His hands were very dirty and sticky from all the painting and glueing so he remembered to go and wash them.

Jennifer had brought something very special for break. She had brought a bag of small chocolate mice, in silver paper wrappers. She laid them on the table. Oliver liked them a lot. The pattern on one of the wrappers was a whiskery mouse face with pink eyes. Oliver loved it.

'Amit and Charlie, go and wash your hands,' said Linda, one of the play-group helpers. 'You're both very grubby. And Jennifer, will you give out the drinks?'

Jennifer jumped up, pleased it was her turn. It was a very special job.

Oliver was left on his own at the table for a few minutes, as he'd washed his hands already. He looked at the row of mice again.

And then Oliver had an idea. Dad's birthday present! Dad would love a chocolate mouse, surely. And if Jennifer has got all those mice, why shouldn't I have just one? thought Oliver. Jennifer's not going to miss it. And I haven't many pennies in my money-box pig.

Oliver looked round the playroom. The helpers and the other children were all busy with drinks and biscuits. No one was looking at him.

Very quickly, before he could stop it, Oliver's hand shot out and grabbed one of the chocolate mice, the one with tiny pink eyes. Somehow the mouse found its way across the room into Oliver's anorak pocket. Oliver hid himself behind all the anoraks and coats hanging up on the pegs. Then he heard a little squeaky voice.

'Eek!' said the voice. It was coming from Oliver's anorak pocket. Oliver realised it must be the mouse, so he took it out of the pocket to have another look at it. It was such a smart mouse, dressed in shiny silvery paper. Oliver knew that Dad would like it.

'Hallo, mouse,' said Oliver, peering closely at the mouse.

'Eek!' said the mouse again. 'I belong to Jennifer, not

you. Please put me back on the table. You stole me. You're a thief!'

'I'm not a thief. I want you for Dad's birthday present,' said Oliver. 'I can't take you back now. Jennifer will know I've —'

'Eek!' said the mouse again, and somehow Oliver didn't want to talk to it any more. He pushed it back into the pocket, and gave it a hard little goodbye squeeze. Then he peeped out from the anoraks to make sure that he could run back to his table without being seen. In seconds he was sitting down with Charlie and Amit, drinking his orange juice. He was even more hot and thirsty than usual, from hiding in the coats by the radiator.

Jennifer came and sat down again at the table by the row of mice. Oliver thought she wouldn't notice that one was missing. But Jennifer did.

'One of my mice has disappeared!' cried Jennifer. 'My best one! It had pink eyes.'

The play-group helpers asked if anyone had seen Jennifer's mouse. Nobody had. The children looked under the tables, but there was no sign of the mouse. Oliver pretended to look as well. Somehow he was beginning to feel very unhappy about the chocolate mouse.

'Have you seen it anywhere, Oliver?' asked Linda. 'You were sitting next to Jennifer.'

'No,' fibbed Oliver. He felt rather scared now as well as unhappy.

'Perhaps you made a mistake, Jennifer,' said Linda kindly. 'Maybe you counted wrong.'

'I didn't,' said Jennifer, tears starting to run down her cheeks. 'I know there were six, because I counted them with my mum. And now there are only five. Look

'– one, two, three, four, five.'

Oliver felt even more alarmed. Then he said quickly: 'I saw where it went – I've just remembered – it ran down a mouse hole.'

'Oh OLIVER,' said Linda. 'I don't think chocolate mice run down mouse holes. I think you're telling me a fib.'

All the children stared at Oliver. Then Amit, who'd been sitting very quietly, jumped up and said: 'I think Oliver took it. I saw him hiding in the anoraks when I was washing my hands.'

'So did I,' said Charlie. 'I saw Oliver's legs.'

Oliver put his thumb in his mouth – and tasted chocolate. When Oliver had squeezed the mouse goodbye it had melted on to his hand.

'Oh OLIVER,' said Linda again, when she saw Oliver's chocolatey hand. 'You naughty little boy.'

Oliver burst into tears. He felt unhappy and ashamed.

'I liked the little mouse so much,' wept Oliver. 'It was for my dad's birthday and I talked to it. I wanted it to give to my dad.'

Oliver went slowly to his anorak to fetch the chocolate mouse, but it was more squashed and melted than ever. It didn't even look like a mouse now, just some rather squidgy chocolate and silver paper.

'Here you are,' muttered Oliver as he gave it back to Jennifer. 'I'm sorry. I won't do it again.'

'I brought them to share,' said Jennifer, 'and I was going to give you one anyway, Oliver. But I'm giving them to my other friends now!'

Oliver was very quiet for the rest of the day. At bedtime Mum said: 'Oliver, whatever is wrong?'

Then Oliver told Mum all about Jennifer's chocolate mouse.

'Oh OLIVER,' said Mum, 'stealing is very wrong and very naughty.'

'Why is it very wrong and very naughty?' said Oliver.

'Because God says so,' said Mum. 'God loves us and has made rules for us to keep, so that we can all be happy. It was wrong to take that mouse from Jennifer, because it was *her* chocolate mouse, not *yours*. You made her sad when you stole it. And telling lies always makes things worse.'

Oliver thought very hard about that. Then he said to God: 'I'm sorry I made Jennifer sad. She's my friend. I'm sorry I stole her chocolate mouse and told lies. I'll try never to do it again.'

Then Oliver said to Mum: 'I know now what I want to buy Dad when we go shopping tomorrow – a chocolate mouse!'

'Oh OLIVER,' said Mum.

Oliver and the baby

Oliver's mum had a friend who dropped in by surprise for tea. Her name was Aunty Brenda, and she brought a baby with her. Oliver felt very cross, because he'd been going to the park and now he couldn't go. It wasn't FAIR.

Oliver knew a bit about babies, because Sam and Charlotte were babies and he loved them very much indeed, but this was a different baby that Oliver had never met before. Its name was Hughie and it was a very big, plump baby. It sat and stared at Oliver out of large, brown eyes.

'Come and talk to Hughie,' said Aunty Brenda to Oliver. She lifted Hughie out of his pram and brought him into the room where the twins were sitting playing on a rug. She sat him in a baby seat on the floor.

'I don't want to,' said Oliver loudly. 'I'd much rather go to the park or play cars with Vimal or paint a picture. I don't like strange babies much, only Sam and Charlotte, and I'm rather busy this afternoon.'

'Come along, Oliver,' said Mum, 'that's not at all polite.'

'All right,' said Oliver. But he'd just thought of a very

naughty idea.

He went and sat down by the baby seat and talked to Hughie very closely.

'Oh, there now,' Oliver heard Aunty Brenda say, 'he's making friends.'

But Oliver wasn't making friends. He was talking very quietly to baby Hughie, who was wearing a smart white jumper.

'I'm a monster,' Oliver was saying, 'and I'm going to eat you up.'

Hughie stared at Oliver.

'I'm a big green hairy scary monster,' said Oliver. 'I'm from outer space. I'm going to send you far away to the stars. GRRRR!!' He pushed teddy bear Bruin at Hughie's face. Hughie went on staring at Oliver.

Oliver sat down by the twins with Bruin and sucked his thumb.

'There,' said Aunty Brenda, 'I knew they'd soon be friends.'

Oliver scowled. But then they all had tea, which was nice. Oliver ate six sandwiches, and after tea Mum said he could go and play.

'Paint something for Aunty Brenda,' suggested Mum.

'Paint the baby,' suggested Aunty Brenda.

Oliver went up to his bedroom and got out his cars. He made a long road of cars along the floor, and then he remembered he wanted to do some painting. But he certainly didn't want to paint a picture of the baby, and anyway, he couldn't find any paper. Then he had another good idea. He'd paint himself instead. He'd paint himself green, then baby Hughie really would think he was a monster and he'd cry and cry and Aunty Brenda would take him home and they'd never come again.

Oliver thought he heard Bruin say: 'Oliver, careful ...'

'Don't FUSS me, Bruin,' said Oliver impatiently. He put Bruin down quickly on the other side of the room. Then he took off most of his clothes. He plastered himself with green finger paint, especially his hands and face, and even his hair.

Then he had another, very naughty idea. Paint the baby, was what Aunty Brenda had said. Well, that's just what I'll do, thought Oliver. And I shan't need any paper for *that*.

Oliver crept down the stairs, hoping that nobody would see him coming. But the house was quiet. Oliver could just hear a murmur of voices from the living room and the tinkle of teacups. Oliver peeped through the half-open door. Hughie was still sitting in his little seat ... The right moment had nearly come for this wonderful jokey trick ... NOW!

Oliver burst into the living room waving his green hands and shouting, 'I'm a monster! I'm a monster!! I'm a bright green monster!! GRRRR!'

Before Mum or Aunty Brenda could stop him, he rushed over to Hughie and put his arms round him and grabbed him and covered his face and his white jumper in green handprints. He was just about to tip up the baby seat as hard as he could when he remembered something. He remembered Bruin telling him to be careful ... So he rocked the baby seat instead – but even so Hughie rolled out on the floor.

Mum and Aunty Brenda leapt out of their chairs, spilling their tea.

'OLIVER!!!' shrieked Aunty Brenda.

'OLIVER!!!' shouted Mum. She grabbed Oliver away from Hughie while Aunty Brenda rescued Hughie

from the floor.

This time Hughie didn't laugh, and nor did Aunty Brenda. Mum looked very cross indeed and Hughie screamed and screamed so loudly that Sam and Charlotte started screaming as well. Oliver suddenly felt frightened at what he'd done. Suppose the paint wouldn't come off Hughie's face and nice white jumper? Mum would never stop being cross. Suddenly Oliver burst into tears as well.

'Stop that noise at once, Oliver,' said Mum firmly, and Aunty Brenda comforted Hughie. Fortunately Hughie hadn't hurt himself at all as the carpet was soft, and the baby seat was very low, near to the floor.

'Oh OLIVER,' said Mum and Aunty Brenda together.

'I was a monster,' explained Oliver, as Mum took Oliver into the kitchen and Aunty Brenda whisked Hughie away into the bathroom. Sam and Charlotte sat in their high chairs. Oliver was sorry he'd made them cry.

'You're not a monster any more,' said Mum. She sounded cross. 'You're an extremely rude and naughty little boy. I'm ashamed of you.'

'I didn't want that baby to come to tea,' muttered Oliver, struggling into a clean jumper. 'And anyway, Aunty Brenda told me to paint the baby. Will they come to tea again?'

'I shouldn't think so,' said Mum. 'You could have hurt Hughie badly.'

'Could I?' said Oliver. There was still green paint on his face. He rubbed his eyes and his nose, sniffing. He hadn't wanted to hurt Hughie. That would have been terrible. Supposing it had been Sam and Charlotte covered in paint and falling on the floor ...

'You must say sorry,' said Mum.

'I don't want to,' said Oliver. 'Will Aunty Brenda be very cross?'

'She might,' said Mum, 'but you must say sorry, to her and to Hughie.'

'Oh, all *right*,' said Oliver. He held Bruin's hand tightly.

Soon Aunty Brenda and Hughie reappeared. Hughie was wearing a clean jumper, one that belonged to Sam. Oliver went over to Hughie. He mouthed a very soft, 'Sorry'.

Then Hughie laughed and chuckled at Oliver. He poked his finger at Oliver's green nose, just like Sam and Charlotte did sometimes when he pulled funny faces at them. Perhaps Hughie wasn't so bad after all.

'I'm sorry I painted Hughie,' mumbled Oliver. He really did feel sorry.

Aunty Brenda said sternly: 'Well, it was naughty of you, wasn't it? Very naughty. I can see you're sorry though, so we'll forget all about it. But I shouldn't ever do it again.'

'No, I won't,' said Oliver, ashamed.

At bedtime Oliver said to God: 'I'm very, VERY sorry I was so naughty. I'll try not to be naughty any more. Please help me to be good.'

The next day Oliver painted a very nice picture of Hughie. He and Mum walked through the park and took it to Aunty Brenda. Mum helped him write on it: 'To my friend Hughie. Love from Oliver the Monster.'

Oliver
and the birthday party

It was nearly time for Oliver's fifth birthday party to begin. Oliver wore a new T-shirt and he felt very excited as he waited for his friends to arrive. Polly was coming, and Vimal, and some other friends too: Scott and Vicky and Darren and Laura and James and Reena and Harry. The twins, Sam and Charlotte, wore their best clothes for the occasion.

'I like parties,' said Oliver, as he helped Mum tie balloons with faces to everyone's chair. He looked at the table. It was full of all sorts of sandwiches and cakes and biscuits. In the centre of the table was a big cake with 'Oliver' written on it in squiggly icing, and five candles. There was red wobbly jelly, and crisps and lemonade.

One plate contained a row of gingerbread people.

'Hallo,' whispered Oliver to the gingerbread people. 'It's my birthday. It's a very special day. God made me five years ago.'

Oliver was sure that he saw the gingerbread wriggle and giggle. He thought he saw one wink at him and say:

'Happy Birthday, Oliver.'

Oliver liked that. He said: 'Thank you for coming to my party.'

Then all Oliver's friends started arriving with presents for Oliver. 'Happy Birthday, Oliver, Happy Birthday,' said everyone.

Oliver liked being given cards and presents. He unwrapped some crayons and a book. Scott gave him a toy car. Vicky gave him a paintbox. Vimal gave Oliver a football. That deserved a big thank you, Oliver decided.

'Oo, THANK YOU, Vimal,' said Oliver. The football bounced out of the wrapping paper just as Oliver started to undo his present from Polly.

'I hope you like it, Oliver,' said Polly, excitedly.

Oliver took a peep, but hardly looked at it. Then he put it to one side very quickly, still in its wrapping, and grabbed the football.

'Say thank you, Oliver,' reminded Mum, busy sorting out drinks.

'I don't want to,' muttered Oliver in a small voice that Mum didn't hear. Polly looked very disappointed, but then there were games to play. Dad put on loud music for Musical Bumps and Pass the Parcel. Oliver hoped he'd win – but Vimal did.

Then it was tea-time and everyone sat up to the table.

'The party's really begun,' thought Oliver happily. He sat opposite Vimal and next to the plate of gingerbread people. He had a quick chat to the fat yellow balloon tied to his chair, just to remind it that it was his birthday.

'Happy Birthday,' said the balloon in a rubbery little voice.

'Thank you,' said Oliver.

At first Polly was sitting near Oliver, then she changed places very quickly and sat next to her friend Laura.

Mum lit the candles on Oliver's cake. Oliver longed for the special moment when he would blow them out.

The party grew noisier and noisier, with music and giggling and shouting. Polly talked to Laura, and took no notice of Oliver. Vimal and Harry and Scott were chattering to each other.

Suddenly Oliver felt shy and not very hungry any more. They've all forgotten about ME, thought Oliver crossly. He so wanted to blow out the candles on his cake. Mum was busy filling jugs and glasses of lemonade. Dad was changing the music on the tape. Just then baby Sam choked and spluttered, and everyone turned to see what was happening.

This was Oliver's chance to disappear and play on his own for a while. While all the other children looked at Sam getting his breath back, Oliver carefully undid the balloon from his chair. He took one of the gingerbread people in the other hand and he wriggled down from his chair. He slithered quietly underneath the table.

Under the table was like being in a special little tent with the tablecloth for walls. It was all crumby and dark and muffled and Oliver could see feet dangling above him. Oliver heard Mum say: 'Leave him alone, he'll come out in a minute.'

'But we're not coming out yet, are we?' said Oliver to the gingerbread person and the balloon face. He made them play with each other and do a little dance. They jigged about together.

'What would you like to eat?' whispered Oliver to the

balloon, pushing his finger into its mouth.

'Careful,' warned the gingerbread person. Its voice was deep and spicy.

'Well blow *me*,' said the balloon. 'I think I'd like a lollipop ... POP!!!' and the balloon burst loudly. Oliver jumped in fright, and grabbed hard at the tablecloth ... and there was a VERY big crash.

All the children shrieked and squealed as jelly and cakes and sandwiches slithered to the floor, and lemonade spilt everywhere.

The twins yelled. Zippy lapped some milk. Oliver crawled out from under the table, wound up in the tablecloth and red in the face. He burst into tears. He held half a piece of gingerbread person in one hand and shreds of yellow balloon in the other.

'My balloon!' roared Oliver. 'It was my special Happy Birthday balloon and it's popped. It played a game with me and now it's broken.'

'Oh OLIVER,' said Mum.

'Oh OLIVER,' said everyone.

It took a very long time to sort out everyone and clear up the mess.

Then Oliver stood on his chair holding a spare balloon. Everyone sang 'Happy Birthday to You', and Oliver blew out the candles on his cake, all in one go! He felt happy.

Oliver sang 'Happy Birthday to Me', and everyone clapped and laughed.

'Thank you, thank you, thank you, thank you,' said Oliver.

They all played some more games and then the party was over.

Polly whispered something shyly in Mum's ear.

'Why, Oliver,' said Mum, 'you haven't looked at

Polly's present yet.'

Oliver slowly undid it. The present was a lovely wooden jigsaw.

'But it wasn't there before,' said Oliver. 'It was just a box. There weren't any pictures. It wasn't an anything.'

'Oh OLIVER,' said Dad. 'You didn't look at it properly. You were in such a hurry you had it upside down. You only saw the underneath!'

'Oh,' said Oliver. He put his thumb in his mouth. 'Sorry, Polly.'

'That's all right,' said Polly. Then Polly and Oliver sat on the floor together and did the jigsaw. It turned into a picture of a train.

'THANK you Polly,' said Oliver, and Polly looked very happy.

Then everyone went home with a party present; a notebook and a pencil and a lollipop and a balloon. Everyone said: 'Thank you for having me.'

'There have been lots and lots of thank yous,' Oliver said to Mum.

'Thank yous make people happy, especially after they give us presents,' said Mum.

At bedtime Oliver said a big thank you to God. He said: 'Thank you, God, for my party and my tea and my balloon and my presents and my friends. And thank you for having me. Goodnight.'

Oliver
and the big green snake

Oliver's mum was busy knitting. She was knitting a big green snake.

'Why are you knitting a snake?' asked Oliver.

'It's to keep the living room door open,' said Mum. 'I shall stuff it when it's finished, then I shall sew a red felt tongue on it. And then it will lie by the door, to stop it slamming and banging and closing when I don't want it to. It will be a very useful door-stop snake.'

The snake was soon finished and it lay on the floor by the door looking very smart. Oliver liked the snake. He wiggled it and waggled it and scared the twins with it.

'You can play with it,' said Mum, 'but it must always go back beside the door. You mustn't ever play with it in the garden. It might get dusty and dirty and spoilt.'

'All right,' said Oliver.

After lunch one hot summer afternoon Mum was busy upstairs with the twins who needed lots of things doing to them at once. Mum was very tired because the twins

were teething and they had been crying all night. She settled the twins and sat down for a rest. She fell asleep ...

Oliver played quietly downstairs with his bricks. He made a house for the big green snake. It was a nice house. It covered the snake except for its head which poked out at one end and looked at Bruin the bear.

Oliver talked to the snake.

'Hallo, Snake,' said Oliver. 'Do you like your house?'

'Yesssss,' said the snake in a snakey sort of voice. 'But I'm very hot and thirsssssty. I'd like to be outdoors having a drink and a bath.'

Bruin shook his head very slowly as if to say: 'No.'

'I'm not allowed to take you outdoors,' said Oliver, remembering what Mum had said, and trying hard not to look at Bruin. Then he thought what fun he and the snake could have in the sunny garden.

'I don't suppose it would matter, just once,' said the snake, softly.

'I don't know ...' said Oliver. 'Oh, all right. But not Bruin, just us.'

Oliver and the snake slipped outside without making a sound.

Then Oliver had an idea. At the far end of the garden he saw the hose lying in a coil under the trees. It was loosely fixed to an outdoor tap, where Dad had been watering the plants and forgotten to undo it.

'Come on, Snake,' said Oliver. 'You can have your drink and a bath. We've got a nice secret hidey-hole down here.'

A cool breeze blew and it was very quiet. Old Mr Jolly was weeding his flower garden on the other side of the fence at number six, The Crescent. But Oliver didn't notice him. He was too busy with the snake.

44

Vimal and Polly were playing in their garden next door at number eight. They came round with Honey to see what Oliver was doing.

'I'm bathing my snake,' explained Oliver in a hoarse whisper. 'He's hot and thirsty. But we've got to be quiet. This is a secret game.'

The hose was difficult to turn on. Oliver tried, and nothing happened. Vimal and Polly had a go, then Oliver tried again. This time a little stream of water came trickling out of the other end. Then the hose began to wriggle about, so they all uncoiled it.

'It's like another snake,' giggled Polly.

'Ssh,' said Oliver.

'Let me have another go,' said Vimal.

Together they wrenched at the tap again, and suddenly a huge jet of water squirted out everywhere. Oliver and Vimal and Polly forgot to be quiet. They squealed and shrieked and they turned the hose on everything they could see. They splashed the snake until it was drenched and sodden. Water poured all over the flowers and trees and the grass.

'And next door!' shouted Polly. 'We can water Mr Jolly's plants!'

'And we can wash the windows!' yelled Vimal. 'And Honey, too!'

'The snake's enjoying this!' said Oliver.

They held the hose between them and swung it towards the house. Water streamed down the windows. Then they turned it over the fence towards old Mr Jolly's garden. There was so much water! Oliver began to feel scared. Even Honey was soaking wet. Perhaps they ought to stop soon ...

'WHATEVER ARE YOU DOING?' said a terribly angry voice, and there was old Mr Jolly appearing over

45

the fence on the other side of Oliver's garden. Mr Jolly didn't look nearly as jolly as usual. The jet of water caught his face and his spectacles flew off his nose. Oliver heard them fall on the path. And all the time Honey barked and barked and barked.

'TURN OFF THAT HOSE AT ONCE,' roared Mr Jolly.

'I can't turn off the tap,' wailed Vimal.

Indoors Oliver's mum heard the breeze slam the living room door. She saw the snake had disappeared. She heard all the commotion and came rushing outside. She ran to the tap and turned the water off.

Everywhere looked very wet and sad. The windows were dripping, and the plants were drowned. Oliver and Polly and Vimal were soaking wet. Polly and Vimal were crying and ashamed when they saw what they'd done, and Oliver was upset and crying too. Honey paddled pools of water everywhere. Poor old Mr Jolly was drenched from head to foot. He couldn't see properly to pick up his broken glasses. And the big green snake was soggy and spoilt. It didn't even look like a snake now, more like a wet woolly sausage.

'Oh OLIVER,' said Mum. She sounded rather tired. She picked up the snake and squeezed water out of it.

Oliver went on crying. Mum was very, very cross with him indeed. Vimal and Polly were sent home with Honey, in disgrace, and then there was a great deal of clearing up to be done.

'Oh OLIVER,' said Mum again. 'You were VERY naughty and disobedient.'

Dad wasn't at all pleased with Oliver. He marched Oliver round next door to say a very big sorry to Mr Jolly for spoiling his nice garden and breaking his spectacles. Oliver scowled and muttered that he was sorry.

Mr Jolly peered fiercely at Oliver over the top of his spare spectacles.

'I should think you are sorry, young man,' said Mr Jolly.

Oliver hung his head and sucked his thumb.

'Well,' said old Mr Jolly, more kindly, 'I suppose I was a little boy like you once. But next time you want to give a snake a bath, I suggest you go to the Zoo, *not* my prize garden.'

'That wasn't too good, was it?' said Bruin later on.

'No,' said Oliver sadly, holding Bruin's furry paw. 'It was bad.'

Polly's mum was good at knitting. She knitted a new big green snake for Oliver's mum. Polly helped stuff it, and Vimal helped stitch on its red felt tongue. The new snake lay by the door and didn't move.

'You've got to stay indoors,' Oliver whispered to the new snake. 'And you must do as you're told. Always. If you don't, there's trouble.'

Then Oliver said very, very quietly to God: 'I'm sorry I was naughty and disobedient. I should have done what I was told. I'm sorry, God. Amen.'

Oliver and the garden zoo

Oliver and Vimal and Polly were playing in Oliver's garden. Their ball went into the garden shed and Vimal ran to fetch it. He found a spider, dangling on a thread. He called the others to come and see it.

'OOO!! ...' said Polly. 'It's huge! It's enormous! It's got hundreds of legs!! OOOO!! I'm scared!'

The spider ran up and down its thread and the children squealed.

Just then Oliver's mum came outside with drinks and biscuits.

Mum laughed when she heard all the fuss and saw the spider.

'It's only a tiny little spider,' she said. 'I expect it's much more frightened of you. You're much, much bigger.'

Then the spider scuttled away somewhere to the top of the shed, and disappeared.

'I've got an idea,' said Polly. 'Let's play zoos. That spider is our first exhibit. It's a wild spider that lives in a shed.'

'We can look for bugs and beetles,' said Vimal, 'and make little houses out of jam jars and boxes and chairs

48

and leaves and twigs.'

'I've got some toy animals,' said Oliver. 'And Zippy can be a tiger.'

He went indoors and returned with an armful of his various animals: his stuffed monkey and a camel, Bruin the bear, the patchwork giraffe and a plastic snake, his lion pyjama case and a money-box pig and a clay model elephant. Oliver put the snake and the camel in his sandpit for a desert, and spread the other toys round the garden.

Then the children hunted all over the garden for live creatures for their zoo. Vimal found a caterpillar under a leaf, and a shiny beetle, and Polly found a ladybird and a wriggling worm.

'I've found a snail,' said Oliver proudly. 'It was under a stone.'

'There are butterflies on that bush,' said Polly. 'They're part of the zoo already, and there are goldfish in the pond, so that's the lake.'

It was rather difficult keeping some of the animals in their houses. Oliver's toy animals didn't move of course, and the goldfish stayed in the pond. The butterflies fluttered round the same bush. But the snail and the caterpillar and the beetle and the worm roamed about. Zippy trampled all over their homes of twigs and grass and leaves, walked in and out of the chairs and boxes, then went to sleep under a bush.

'That's the tiger's cage,' said Polly.

'Can I be the zoo keeper?' said Oliver. 'I'll be in charge of all the animals, and I can wear my peaked cap.'

'All right,' said Vimal. 'I'll let the people in at the zoo gate. I'll take the money and give tickets.'

'I'm in charge of feeding the animals,' said Polly. 'We

must have pretend food – petals and grass and pebbles and things – and water.'

The children played zoos all day. They asked Oliver's mum to help them with the spelling, and wrote notices for the animals. Some of the notices said: 'DO NOT FEED THE ANIMALS'. The one on the shed read: 'VERY DANGEROUS SPIDER'.

Oliver's mum brought the twins to visit the zoo, and Polly and Vimal's mum came round from next door. Even Mr Jolly from the other next door bought a ticket over the fence.

Oliver liked the snail he'd found very much. He liked its little horns, and the way it carried its house on its back, and the silver trail it left behind as it crept along. Oliver lay down on his tummy and looked at the snail through the grass.

'You're very nice, Mr Snail,' said Oliver in delight.

'I know I'm nice,' said the snail in a gluey sort of voice. 'God made me very slow though. I can't run about as fast as you. It's good of you to stop and talk. Will you be my friend?'

'Yes, please,' said Oliver. But the snail moved away, and Oliver felt rather disappointed. He hoped the snail would come back again.

When Dave next door came home from work he visited the zoo. He looked for the very dangerous spider which had vanished out of sight, and he made monkey noises at the monkey, and pretended to feed it with a bus ticket. Polly and Vimal shrieked with delight, but Oliver said severely: 'You must feed the animals properly in my zoo.'

Oliver's Dad inspected the zoo as well. Then it was time for the zoo to close because it was evening, and Polly and Vimal had to go home.

'Bedtime, Oliver,' said Mum. 'It's time to clear away now.'

Oliver didn't want to go to bed, but he did as he was told and carried all his toy animals upstairs. There was a lot to carry.

Mum followed soon afterwards. She saw a lot of rumpled humps and bumps under the bedclothes.

'You're in bed quickly, Oliver,' said Mum. 'Whatever have you got in bed with you?'

Oliver emerged from among all his toy animals. He was holding Bruin and he still wore his clothes and his peaked zoo keeper's cap.

'That's our zoo,' explained Oliver. 'I can't wear my pyjamas because they have to stay in my pyjama case to make the lion nice and fat.'

'Oh dear,' sighed Mum. Then she looked inside a small, open cardboard box, in bed with all the toy animals, and she said: 'OLIVER – THERE'S A SNAIL IN YOUR BED!!'

'I know,' said Oliver. 'He's my friend, and he's rather lonely.'

'Oh OLIVER,' said Mum. 'You can't take a snail to bed with you, even if it is your friend. It must go back in the garden.'

Oliver put his thumb in his mouth and sulked.

'It's *my* snail,' said Oliver. 'It's my friendly snail, and I found him, and he's in my zoo. God made him nicely, so I've got to look after him.'

'But Oliver,' explained Mum gently, sitting down on the edge of the bed, 'having a snail in bed with you isn't the best way to look after it, at all. God likes us to look after his creatures and animals properly. Your snail will be very hot and unhappy. It will be much much happier out in the garden in the cool grass with

all the other snails.'

'Oh,' sniffed Oliver. 'All right.'

'Tell you what,' said Dad, coming into Oliver's room, 'I think there's something else that's come to join your zoo, out in the garden. Let's take the snail with us and see what's there.'

Dad put on Oliver's zoo keeper hat which made Oliver laugh and cheer up. They went downstairs into the garden. It was getting dark. And there on the lawn was a hedgehog!

'I'm the zoo keeper now,' said Dad. 'But you can feed the hedgehog, Oliver. It might enjoy some of Zippy's food.'

Oliver liked the hedgehog very much. It had a lot of prickles. He put the snail under some cool leaves, then he and Mum gave the hedgehog a saucer of cat food. The hedgehog snuffled and sniffed and ate some.

'Now it really *is* bedtime,' said Mum firmly.

Before he went to sleep Oliver said his prayers. He said to God:

'Thank you, God, for my zoo. Thank you for the snail and the hedgehog and all the animals. Thank you for all your creatures. Help me to look after them properly. Amen. Goodnight.'

Oliver and the sand-castle

Oliver went to the seaside for the day, with Mum and Dad and Charlotte and Sam. Polly and Vimal and Honey came too. Bruin stayed at home.

'We've got lots of luggage,' said Oliver. They'd brought a picnic lunch and drinks and a big rug and a ball and swimming things and buckets and spades. Polly had a yellow spade and Vimal had a beautiful blue bucket. Oliver had a new, little red spade. He was very, very proud of it.

At the beach the sun shone and the sea sparkled.

'It's lovely,' said Polly, feeling the warm sand on her bare toes.

'I'm going to swim,' said Vimal, looking at the blue water.

'I'm going to dig,' said Oliver, holding his little red spade tightly.

There was plenty of time to splash and swim and paddle and play ball.

Oliver said to God: 'I'm ever so happy. You have made a lovely day.'

Oliver looked at his new spade. It winked back at him in the sunlight.

'I'm going to make lots and lots of holes,' said Oliver.

'So am I,' said Polly. 'I love my yellow spade.'

She ran down to the water's edge with Oliver to dig a long river. Vimal filled his bucket with water to put in the holes that Oliver dug. Then Oliver covered Dad in sand. He and Vimal sat on top of Dad together. They looked so funny that Mum took a photograph and the twins squealed and shrieked.

When Oliver had uncovered Dad again he said very quietly to the red spade: 'You're very good at digging. We'll build a big sand-castle later on.'

The tide was a long way out.

'We'd better have that swim before the water disappears,' joked Dad.

Swimming was fun. Honey enjoyed swimming too. Then it was lunch-time.

After the picnic Oliver's dad and Polly went to fetch some ice creams.

Oliver whispered to the little red spade: 'We'll build that big sand-castle now.'

'About time too,' grumbled the spade. 'I've been watching you all eating and drinking. I thought we'd never get started.'

The spade dug an excited little hole as Oliver began to build the castle. Vimal made some sand-pies with his bucket to go round the outside. Polly and Dad came back with delicious ice creams for everyone. After a while Polly wailed: 'My spade! It's gone! It's disappeared!'

The yellow spade had vanished. There was no sign of it anywhere.

'Maybe you took it with you when you went to get the ice creams,' suggested Oliver's mum. So Oliver's dad took Polly back to see if it was there – but it

55

wasn't. Polly was upset and cried, so Oliver's dad set off along the beach to look for it.

'Perhaps another boy or girl has found it,' said Oliver's mum. 'But I'm sure Oliver will let you share his spade until we find yours.'

'Can I?' said Polly, sniffing and looking longingly at Oliver's spade.

'No,' said Oliver, digging hard. 'Not yet. It's my spade, and we're both very busy just now.'

'*Please*, Oliver,' said Polly sadly.

'NO,' said Oliver angrily. 'It's *mine*.'

'Only for a minute,' said Polly, and she tried to grab the spade out of Oliver's hand. Oliver held on furiously, but as they both pulled, the spade hit Polly's face hard.

Oliver thought he heard the little red spade say: 'Ouch! Mind what you're doing! You're going to hurt Polly,' but it was too late. Polly screamed out, holding her face and crying again. Sand flew everywhere. The twins screeched. Vimal sat down in surprise on his carefully made sand-pies. The castle broke into ruins.

'It's *my* spade, it's *mine*,' sobbed Oliver. 'It likes ME best.'

Dad heard the fuss and came back quickly. He took the spade away from Oliver while Mum brushed the twins down. Then she brushed Polly down and put some cream on the bruise on Polly's face. When Oliver saw the bruise he sobbed even more loudly.

'Oh OLIVER,' said Mum. 'That was very, very naughty indeed. You've hurt Polly because you were being so unkind and selfish. You must say sorry, and share your spade, just for a little while.'

'But it was mine,' said Oliver. He put his thumb in his mouth and sulked. Suddenly he wanted Bruin.

'Come on, old chap,' said Dad. 'That sand-castle's never going to get built before the tide comes in.'

'Come ON!' said Vimal impatiently. 'You can share my bucket, Oliver. We'll go and find some seaweed and shells to decorate the castle.'

Oliver scowled again. But he did like Vimal's blue bucket.

'Oh *all right*,' said Oliver, remembering to try and be good.

So they set to work. Polly, and Oliver's spade, worked quickly. Oliver had a turn again – and this time he remembered to hand the spade back to Polly without any fuss. Honey worked hard too – she dug and dug as if she was searching for a bone. Then she went to sleep on the rug. Vimal and Oliver made more small sand-castles together with the bucket. Then they rushed off and filled the bucket with seaweed and shells. Between them they'd made a wonderful castle.

'Thank you for lending me your spade, Oliver,' said Polly. She suddenly thought of her own yellow spade and wondered where it could possibly be.

All the time the tide was creeping in over the sand. The waves were getting rougher. Then suddenly Vimal said: 'Look!'

They all looked – and there was Polly's spade!

'Hooray!' everyone shouted, and Honey shook sea water all over them.

'You left it by the edge of the water,' said Oliver's mum.

The yellow spade was coming in on the waves. But it was still quite a long way out, and was difficult to reach. It bobbed away from Mum and Dad. It was too far away for Polly or Vimal or Oliver to paddle to it because of the rough waves.

Then Oliver had a very good idea. He said: 'Honey can get it! Wake up, Honey!'

Oliver's spade gave Honey a little prod and she woke up. She splashed into the sea and soon rescued the yellow spade, draped in seaweed. She swam back with it in her mouth.

'Thank you, Oliver! Thank you, Honey!' said Polly happily.

'The sea took it and brought it back,' said Oliver's dad. 'It must have caught round some rocks or a breakwater where we couldn't see it.'

Then the sea rushed in and the children stood on top of the castle. Polly leant proudly on her yellow spade and draped the seaweed round her neck. Vimal put his blue bucket on Oliver's head. Oliver whispered to his little red spade: 'Sharing you wasn't so bad after all.'

He and Vimal held the spade high above their heads, as the castle collapsed around them. It was fun!

By bedtime Oliver was so sleepy he could hardly keep his eyes open. But he said to God: 'Thank you for a lovely day at the seaside, God. I'm sorry I hurt Polly's face. Help me to remember to share. Amen.'

Oliver
and the thunderstorm

One hot day Oliver was riding his trike round the garden and playing with Zippy, when a big, fat raindrop hit him on the nose.

'Oh!' said Oliver, surprised. 'Where have you come from, Mr Raindrop?'

'I've come from that dark, heavy cloud,' said the raindrop. 'Some of my friends are up there too and they'll be coming down in a minute.'

Then the fat raindrop melted away in the hot sun.

Oliver looked up into the sky. The sky had been blue until a few minutes ago, but he could see the dark, heavy cloud, and a few more drops of rain made spots on the path. There was a faint rumbling sound in the distance.

'Oliver,' called Mum, 'put your trike away and come indoors before you get wet. I'm just settling the twins for their afternoon nap.'

The sky grew darker and darker. This time the sun went in behind the dark cloud. Oliver went in too. He went up to his bedroom to find Bruin and his other indoor toys. As he rummaged through his things, some books slid from the shelf with a bump, and a heap of cars fell out of their box with a crash.

'Oh, you are noisy toys today,' said Oliver, putting his hands over his ears. He decided to play with the bricks and make a tall tower to reach the sky. It was hot and stuffy and quite dark in the bedroom, but nice and quiet now. Oliver lay on his tummy putting one brick slowly and carefully on top of another, pretending the tower was going up and up past the trees, into the clouds, into space ...

Crash!!! Oliver's tower fell down round him with a clatter.

'Bother!' said Oliver, and started to rebuild the bricks.

But then he realised that he could still hear a noise, a tumbling, bangy noise that wasn't the books falling down, and it wasn't the cars rattling and crashing, and it wasn't the bricks. The noise was outdoors – it was thunder. Then Mum came into Oliver's room.

'Why did you turn my light on and off again?' said Oliver.

'I didn't,' said Mum. 'That was a flash of lightning.'

'It's thunderstorming,' said Oliver. 'Will it get noisier?'

'It might,' said Mum. 'And I think it's going to rain quite hard soon. There've been lots of heavy drops.'

'I know,' said Oliver. 'There was a big fat raindrop and he hit me on the nose and said that all his friends were coming too.'

The thunder rolled again, louder, this time.

'I should think the fat raindrop was right,' said Mum.

Suddenly a wind blew up outside. There was

another flash of lightning and a big bang of thunder.

'Ouch!' said Oliver. He sidled up to Mum and sucked his thumb. 'I don't like thunderstorms any more,' said Oliver. 'Nor does Bruin.'

'Come on, Oliver,' said Mum. 'Let's switch the light on and rebuild that tower you're making. Storms are quite exciting.'

Then there was another bang and a crash, with a flash that made Oliver jump. The bricks clattered down again, and Bruin fell over. And then the rain came! It seemed as if it was falling out of the sky in great waves. Oliver had never seen such rain. Bruin watched the rain too.

'The fat raindrop has got a lot of friends!' said Oliver.

There was hail too, little white stones hitting the window, while all the time the thunder banged and crashed and the wind still blew and blew. Every now and then there was another flash of lightning.

'Go away, storm!' shouted Oliver. 'Go away, rain-drops!'

'Woosh,' said the raindrops, as they streamed down the window, 'you can't stop us, Oliver.'

Suddenly Oliver felt frightened of the storm. There was no way to stop it. It was too big and bright and noisy. He sat on Mum's lap.

'I wish it would go away,' said Oliver. 'It's a very scary storm. I don't like it.'

BANG!! CRASH!! Oliver thought his bedroom was shaking.

'It's mostly noise,' said Mum. 'Let's read a story together and forget about the silly old storm.'

'I don't like it!' wailed Oliver, and disappeared under a cushion. But he could still hear the thunder.

In between bangs Oliver emerged from the cushion and said: 'Can God stop the thunderstorm?'

'God is in charge of all the weather,' said Mum, above the noise of the wind and the rain. 'Once there was a big storm at sea and Jesus' friends were afraid. Jesus told the storm to stop, and it did. When God wants the thunderstorm to stop – it will. God is in control of everything.'

Oliver disappeared under the cushion again and he said to God: 'Hallo God, it's your friend Oliver again. I hope you can hear me. I don't like this scary storm very much. I feel rather frightened. Please help me not to be afraid, and please stop the storm as soon as you can.'

There was another noise outside the bedroom door. Oliver could only just hear it because it was a very small noise at first, then it grew louder ... the door pushed open with a meow ...

'Zippy!' said Oliver.

Mum opened the door, and in came Zippy. He was soaking wet. His fur stood out in damp spikes and there were raindrops dripping from his whiskers. He looked very frightened.

'Oh, poor Zippy!' said Mum. 'He's been out in the storm. Come on, Oliver, let's dry him. Cats hate being wet, and he might catch a cold.'

Mum found an old towel and they rolled Zippy up in it. Zippy's head stuck out at one end of the towel and his tail poked out at the other.

'Thank you for helping me,' purred Zippy. 'I was a bit frightened.'

'That's all right, Zippy,' whispered Oliver. 'I was too, just a bit.'

Oliver began to get used to the noise of the storm, and even started to forget about it as he rubbed and

rubbed the cat. Soon Zippy lay clean and dry on Oliver's lap. Then Oliver said: 'The storm's going away.'

The room grew lighter and the wind died down. There were some little rumbles of thunder but they were dying away. The lightning had stopped.

'I didn't even notice,' said Oliver. 'Zippy did look scared, didn't he? I'm not frightened any more now.'

Mum said: 'Perhaps you forgot about being frightened when you were busy helping Zippy not to be frightened.'

'Perhaps,' said Oliver. Then he said: 'Did the twins mind the storm?'

'I made sure of that,' said Mum. 'They're not a bit frightened. They were fast asleep – all the time. They missed it – every flash and bang!'

'Perhaps God will send another storm one day,' said Oliver.

'Oh OLIVER,' said Mum.

When Oliver said his prayers that night he said to God: 'Thank you for the exciting, scary storm. Thank you for helping me not to be afraid.'

Oliver and the hard sum

Oliver had just started going to school. He liked it very much.

'Is it time for school?' said Oliver, coming into the kitchen one breakfast time. 'Can we go now? I've been awake a long, long time and I'm wearing my school-bag. I'm all ready.'

'Well, I'm not all ready,' said Mum, without turning round from the cooker. 'Everything's going wrong this morning. The alarm clock didn't go off and Dad's late for work, and the toast has burnt, and I've spilt a bottle of milk, and Charlotte has just splashed orange juice all over her clean dress. You'll have to help me, Oliver. You can spread the bread for your packed lunch.'

Then Mum turned and looked at Oliver.

'Oh OLIVER,' said Mum. 'You're not being at all helpful. You're still in your pyjamas and dressing-gown! You can't go to school like that! I've got the twins to see to – and where are all your things to go in your bag? Where are your shoes?'

'Oliver,' called Dad from the front path, 'can you help me a moment? I've got lots of things to take to the car and I'm late.'

Oliver grumbled to himself. He didn't want to help. He went up to his bedroom and he grumbled to his teddy bear Bruin.

'We just want to go to school, don't we?' said Oliver. 'Helping's boring.'

'But your mum's very busy,' said Oliver's teddy bear Bruin. 'She'd like you to help. You could get dressed for a start.'

'Oh be quiet,' said Oliver crossly. But he found his trousers and his socks and shoes and started putting them on.

'That's better,' said Bruin. 'Your mum will help you with your tie. But don't forget to spread the bread for your packed lunch.'

'Can't you help?' said Oliver to Bruin.

'I've helped you already,' said Bruin. 'I've told you what to do. And I don't like getting butter on my paws. Now go and have your breakfast and pack your school bag.'

'Oh ALL RIGHT,' said Oliver.

Oliver and Bruin just managed not to be late for school.

Oliver's classroom was always very busy. This morning the children were working in turns in different groups. There was painting, and the playhouse, and counters and numbers, and dressing-up and writing news, and playing musical instruments, and cutting out.

Oliver sat at the table with all the counters and number games. He held Bruin on his lap. There were some numbers and shapes and coloured counters to match, and Oliver tried to remember exactly what he had to do with them.

One of the older children, called Jack, was writing something at Oliver's table. He was drawing numbers and putting them into squares in a book.

'I'm doing sums,' explained Jack. 'They're hard. This one is very hard.'

'Oh,' said Oliver. He wished he was old enough to do a hard sum. He looked at what Jack was doing and tried to copy. He wrote some squiggly numbers on a piece of paper. But it didn't look like Jack's hard sum.

It was too difficult. Hard sums are *hard*, thought Oliver, and he soon gave up. He looked instead at all the coloured counters. They were nice bright colours. It seemed rather a waste just to count with them. By now Oliver had completely forgotten what he was supposed to be doing with them, anyway. He suddenly thought he'd like to be at home. He put his thumb in his mouth. Then he remembered that he could ask God to help him with everything. That meant hard sums too. So Oliver said to God: 'I don't know what to do, God. Can you help me please?'

He wondered if God would answer him. Then he looked for his teacher.

Oliver's teacher was called Miss Harrison. Oliver liked her very much. She was young and pretty and kind. But she was very busy just now trying to help all the children in turn, and mop up some spilt paint, and remember whose turn it was to clean out the hamster's cage.

Oliver pushed the counters around the table into patterns. That was interesting for a while, but it got boring. Then Oliver had an idea.

'Let's play tiddly-winks,' said Oliver very softly to Bruin.

'No, that's naughty,' Oliver thought he heard Bruin

whisper back, but Oliver didn't listen. He looked again at Miss Harrison. She was hearing some children read to her at the other end of the classroom.

He flipped a red counter quietly across the table. It landed on Jack's hard sum, and Jack giggled and joined in.

'Ssh,' whispered Jack, 'don't make a noise, or Miss Harrison will hear.' He flipped a blue counter on to the floor. A green one went into the air. Soon the other children were throwing and shooting counters in all directions, like a coloured hailstorm. Then suddenly a yellow one caught a little girl called Anna on her face near her eye.

Anna screamed out and said she'd tell her mum, and Oliver disappeared under the table.

'You didn't help me, God,' said Oliver sadly. 'I expect you were too busy.'

Miss Harrison came over, and when Oliver emerged from under the table she said: 'Oh JACK, oh OLIVER,' and wore a *very* stern face. Oliver snivelled and cried and sobbed and said he wanted to go home.

'I couldn't do my sums,' wept Oliver. 'They were too hard. I didn't know what to do. I could only make squiggles. I didn't mean to hurt Anna.'

Anna sniffed and said she was all right really and she wouldn't tell her mum after all. Oliver felt very glad about that.

'Let's start again,' said Miss Harrison. 'You need some help, Oliver. Let me sit down with you and show you what to do.'

Oliver beamed. He was being helped after all! It was Miss Harrison helping him instead of God, but perhaps that didn't matter. Oliver was soon busy doing all sorts of interesting counting games. Then Miss Harrison said: 'Why, I nearly forgot. I need a helper for the hamster's cage. It's *your* turn today, Oliver! Can you help me very sensibly?'

Oliver enjoyed helping. He tried to have a little chat with the hamster but its cheeks were full of food, so it couldn't talk.

At bedtime Oliver cuddled Bruin and said to Mum and Dad: 'I was a helper today. Miss Harrison helped me with my hard sum and then I helped her to clean out the hamster's cage. I asked God to help me but nothing happened. I expect he was busy.'

'God always hears us, and he *did* help you,' smiled Mum. 'When Jesus lived on this earth he was always helping people. But now he uses *our* hands and feet to help each other. He used Miss Harrison to help *you*, and he used *you* to help Miss Harrison.'

Oliver was pleased that God had used his hands and feet to help his teacher. Perhaps tomorrow they could help Mum and Dad if Mum burnt the toast again and Dad was late for work. He said very sleepily to God: 'Thank you for helping me. Please use my hands and feet. Goodnight.'

Oliver
and the football boots

Oliver's grandma was coming by train to stay. Oliver felt very excited.

'Grandma will see how much you've grown,' said Mum. 'She'll say: "Oh OLIVER, *haven't* you grown?!" '

'I'm very big now,' said Oliver proudly. 'I shall be as big as Polly and Vimal soon. I wish I was as clever as they are, then I could make a special present for Grandma or do something extra nice for her. Vimal's ever so good at reading and writing and kicking a ball, and Polly's learning to sew, and she can read too. I wish I could read properly.'

Mum and Dad were clever too, thought Oliver. Dad had just been putting up some new wallpaper to decorate Oliver's bedroom, and Mum was always cooking yummy cakes and biscuits. It must be nice to be big.

Oliver tried to think of something special and nice that he could do for Grandma. He could draw her a picture – but Grandma had got a lot of his drawings already. He could plant her some seeds – but seeds took a long time to grow. He didn't know what to do.

Then Oliver had an idea. He would make Grandma a secret surprise that nobody else had ever thought of. But first of all he played football in the park with Vimal, when Dave took them there to have a game.

'Come on, Oliver,' said Vimal, 'I'll show you. Watch me!'

But Oliver kept missing the ball and falling over.

'Try wearing my football boots,' said Vimal, but Oliver couldn't walk in them. They were much too big, and Oliver and Vimal giggled.

'You're good boots,' said Oliver to the boots as he took them off.

'Oh we *are*,' said the boots, shuffling about. '*We're* footballers.'

'Will you help me to be a footballer?' asked Oliver.

But the boots had walked away on Vimal's feet.

Oliver went back to Polly and Vimal's house. Polly was sewing.

'Sewing's hard,' said Polly. 'I keep pricking my finger. Knitting's better. But you have to do it right, or it all unravels.'

She showed Oliver how you did knitting, on two special needles. Oliver went on planning his surprise.

The day before Grandma arrived Mum was very busy, as she had to get Grandma's room ready and do some extra cooking. So she didn't really notice exactly what Oliver was doing, as he was playing very quietly in his room, and getting his crayons and paper out, although it was a fine day. She didn't notice him take a ball of wool from her knitting basket, and she didn't notice him putting some flour into a little toy bucket.

'Are you all right, Oliver?' asked Mum. She'd finished Grandma's room and started cooking things in the kitchen.

'Oh yes,' said Oliver. 'I'm just very busy getting ready for Grandma.'

Mum laughed, and went upstairs to finish tidying Grandma's bedroom.

The next day Grandma arrived on the train. Mum and Dad and Oliver and the twins all went to meet her.

'Oh OLIVER,' said Grandma, '*haven't* you grown?!'

'I've got a surprise for you,' said Oliver excitedly, and hugged and kissed Grandma. 'It's a very secret surprise.'

'I can't wait,' smiled Grandma, kissing and hugging the twins too.

After tea Oliver said: 'The secret surprise is nearly ready now, Grandma. But there's one more thing I've got to do ...'

Everyone waited, and then Oliver reappeared. He was carrying a plate of flour and water shapes that were rather wet and grey and gooey. On his head was a pile of tangled red wool, slipping over his eyes. He had Vimal's big boots on his feet. His hands were wet and sticky.

Mum and Dad and Grandma laughed and laughed and laughed, until the tears ran down their cheeks. Sam and Charlotte stared, open-mouthed, and then they crowed and gurgled and clapped their hands.

'Oh Oliver,' said Grandma. 'That *was* funny! What a wonderful surprise.'

But Oliver didn't laugh. He was extremely cross.

'It's not funny,' said Oliver. 'It was a secret surprise for Grandma, and I've made her cakes, and knitted her a hat, and you've spoilt it all. You shan't see the rest of the surprise now. Not ever.'

'Oh yes we will,' said Dad, trying to look serious. 'I can't wait.'

'Please, Oliver,' said Grandma. 'Let's see the rest of your surprise.'

'Oh all RIGHT!' said Oliver. 'But you've got to watch the garden.'

He cheered up and went outside, clumping along in Vimal's big boots.

'Go on, boots,' said Oliver. 'You've got to help me.'

But the boots didn't answer.

Everyone watched through the window, and Oliver kicked his football as hard as he could. One of Vimal's boots said, 'Ouch!' and flew off Oliver's foot into the air. The ball flew into the air too, but not where Oliver meant it to go. It hit Grandma's bedroom window ... and broke the glass.

'Oh OLIVER,' said Mum and Dad and Grandma. They all stopped laughing, and rushed upstairs to look at the damage. As Mum opened the bedroom door she gasped: 'Oliver! You've been trying do some decorating!'

There were pieces of scribbly coloured paper stuck all over the wall.

'Oh OLIVER,' said Mum, 'whenever did you do that? It wasn't there earlier when I came in.'

'Enough is enough,' said Dad. 'Go and clear up all this mess AT ONCE.'

'But I wanted to be grown up and clever like everyone else,' wept Oliver. 'I wanted to do something special for Grandma. I tried to be really, really clever like Polly and Vimal and you and Mum, all at once. It was a secret surprise but it didn't work.'

'Oh OLIVER,' said Grandma, cuddling him tightly.

'You don't have to be clever for people to love you or think you're special. You're YOU, Oliver. You're not Polly or Vimal or Mum or Dad – or me. You're you, just as God made you. It's who you are, not what you do that matters.'

'But everything all goes wrong,' said Oliver sadly.

'Things do, sometimes,' said Grandma, 'but God helps us put them right again.'

Grandma and Mum and Dad helped Oliver to clear up the mess. Then Oliver sat on Grandma's lap and she wore the tangly, loopy red woolly hat that Oliver had knitted. It looked very funny indeed, and they laughed and laughed together.

'Polly uses big needles,' said Oliver. 'But I knitted it on my fingers.'

While Grandma's window was being repaired, Oliver chatted to Grandma about all sorts of things. They looked at a lot of story picture books together. And one day Oliver and Grandma discovered that he could very nearly read!

'Just like Polly and Vimal,' said Oliver proudly.

'No,' laughed Grandma, 'just like Oliver. There's no one quite like you, Oliver! And there's time for you to learn to do all sorts of things.'

Grandma heard Oliver say his prayers. He said to God: 'Thank you God for making me ME. Please help me with the things I can't do yet, and when everything goes wrong. Amen.'

Oliver and the pumpkin

It was Harvest Festival day at Oliver's school. All the children were bringing boxes and parcels of fruit and vegetables to school, and tins of food and jars of jam.

'We bring our gifts to say thank you to God for all the good things we have to eat,' explained Miss Harrison. 'And then the gifts are given to old people or ill people.'

Oliver and Mum put some carrots and tomatoes and a tin of peas and an apple and a pear into a box. They made it into a basket with a handle. The basket was decorated with tissue paper and cellophane, with a pretty ribbon on the top. Oliver was very pleased with his harvest parcel.

'I wonder what Polly and Vimal are taking,' said Oliver excitedly on the morning of Harvest Festival, just as he and Mum and the twins were setting off to school. 'They wouldn't tell me. They said it was a secret. But I think my basket will be the best.'

'It doesn't really matter whose is the best,' smiled Mum. 'As long as you're giving it to say thank you to God.'

Oliver carried his harvest basket very carefully along

the road. But just as they reached the school gate, Oliver was in such a hurry to get into school and show everyone his harvest present, that he tripped on the twins' pushchair and fell over. The basket flew out of his hand and everything fell out. One of the tomatoes squished and the apple rolled into the road. Oliver accidentally trod on the basket.

'Oh OLIVER,' said Mum.

'Ohhh,' wailed Oliver, clutching a small carrot, 'my harvest present, my harvest present! It's all spoilt.'

Oliver sat in the middle of the school path and howled.

Mum gathered up all the things from Oliver's basket and tried to put it together. But the ribbon had come off and the tissue paper had torn. And the special Harvest Festival morning started very soon.

'Dry your eyes, Oliver,' said Mum. 'I know what we'll do. I'll take the basket home and mend it, very quickly, and bring it back. You tell Miss Harrison what's happened.'

Oliver snivelled and sniffed. He felt very sad. All the other children would have something lovely to take for Harvest Festival except him.

'Will you be quick, and can I take the carrot?' said Oliver, still clutching the little carrot in his hand.

'Yes, of course,' said Mum. 'But hurry, or we're going to be late. Off you go, and I'll bring your present back as soon as I can.'

Harvest Festival was all ready to happen in the school hall, which looked bright and cheerful. The children had been very busy. Oliver's class had painted a field full of yellow corn. Vimal's class had made a picture of a rosy apple tree. Polly's class had cooked

78

some real bread.

Oliver sat with Polly and Vimal near the back of the hall so that Mum could hand him his basket when she'd mended it, without any fuss. He looked all round, holding the little carrot very tightly in his hand. He hoped Mum wouldn't be long. The other children had such lovely boxes and parcels, all wrapped up to look as pretty as possible.

That was when Oliver saw what Polly and Vimal had brought – a giant pumpkin. And it was so big it even had a chair all to itself!

Oliver couldn't stop looking at the enormous pumpkin. It was a beautiful deep orangey colour with a nice chunky stalk. Oliver looked at his thin little carrot and felt sad. He wished he had a giant pumpkin to give to God. And where was Mum? She'd promised she wouldn't be long.

The children all sang some harvest songs to say thank you to God.

Oliver fidgeted and scratched a mouth and eyes on the carrot with his fingernail. It looked funny. There was even a little bump for a nose.

'Hallo, carrot,' whispered Oliver, pretending he was singing.

'Hallo,' said the carrot, 'isn't this fun? I like singing to God.'

'Will my mum be here soon, do you think?' asked Oliver anxiously.

'Oh, I'm sure she will,' said the carrot. 'But you've got me for the time being, haven't you? We can sing to God together.'

'Well, yes,' said Oliver, 'but you're rather small and thin, you see.'

'Small? Thin? Me?' chuckled the carrot. 'That

doesn't really matter, not one bit, not when you're as nice and juicy as me. God will like me being given to him, just as I am. After all, he made me that way.'

'Oh,' said Oliver, staring at the carrot. Then Oliver started to laugh too. The carrot had such a funny face. And then he realised that all the other children had sat down again. There was silence in the school hall. Everyone was staring at Oliver in amazement as he stood there all on his own talking to the carrot.

'*OLIVER*,' hissed Vimal, leaning across the pumpkin. '*OLIVER – sit down*.'

'*OLIVER*,' nudged Polly, tugging at Oliver's jersey, '*OLIVER – ssh*.'

Then Oliver thought he heard the pumpkin speak to the carrot.

'I'm much bigger than you,' it said in a deep voice. 'Skinny!'

'Oh no you're not,' said the carrot. 'Fatty!'

And somehow the carrot and the pumpkin both rolled on to the floor. All the children laughed and giggled at Oliver. He felt silly and shy. He didn't like everyone staring at him.

'Oh OLIVER,' said a familiar voice, and there was Mum, breathless from hurrying. She hastily gave Oliver his mended basket.

Miss Harrison told the children to settle down again. Vimal and Polly lifted the pumpkin back on to its chair. When it was time to take up all the gifts they carried it between them up to the front of the hall. But Oliver hastily popped the little carrot into his pocket.

'You've caused enough trouble already, you and that pumpkin,' said Oliver. 'You stay there for a bit and be an ordinary carrot again.'

He enjoyed taking his basket up to the front of the

hall, and forgot all about the little carrot for the time being. The children all sang another thank you song to God, and then they all said a prayer. They said: 'Thank you God for the sun and the rain that make the crops grow. Thank you for all the good things we have to eat. Please help all the children everywhere who don't have enough to eat, and teach us to share.'

'I liked Harvest Festival,' said Oliver to Mum at bedtime. 'It was nice saying thank you to God for all the food. Do you know? Polly and Vimal's pumpkin was very, very big. It even had a chair to itself!'

'It doesn't matter which is the biggest,' smiled Mum. 'Polly and Vimal's pumpkin was very, very lovely, but God will use everything that was given to him, all those harvest gifts that were given to share.'

Then Mum said: 'Where did you put that little carrot that you took in to school first of all, on its own?'

'I was hungry after all that singing and talking to God and looking at all those things to eat,' said Oliver. 'And the carrot fell on the floor. So I washed it under the tap at break. And then I ate it!'

'Oh OLIVER!' said Mum.

Oliver and the foggy frog

It was a dull, foggy, wintry afternoon. Dad had come home earlier than usual that day from work and he collected Oliver from school for a surprise. The car had gone wrong and was at the garage being mended, so they had to walk. Dad pretended he didn't know the way home from school.

'Tell me which roads to go along, Oliver,' said Dad. 'And tell me where the letter-box is. There's an important letter to post on the way.'

Oliver didn't answer. He was tired. He wished they were going home by car. He trailed along the pavement dragging his school-bag.

The fog was quite thick and swirly. Everything sounded muffled.

At the end of the road the houses were bigger and more spread apart, with high gates and thick hedges. Oliver could just see through the hedge that one of the houses, the one near the letter-box, had a pond in the front garden.

Suddenly Oliver had a surprise. He said: 'Oh look – there's a frog!'

The frog was small and greeny-brown with long legs.

It sat on the path under a hedge, and didn't move.

Oliver liked the frog. He bent down to talk to it.

'Hallo, foggy frog,' said Oliver. 'Why are you sitting on the pavement?'

'I'm a bit lost,' croaked the frog, so quietly that only Oliver could hear it. 'I'm on my way back to my pond before someone treads on me.'

'You can get through the hedge, just there – there's a little hole,' said Oliver, and the frog gave a little jump, and was gone.

'I like the frog,' said Oliver. 'Can I post the letter now?'

'Hold it carefully,' said Dad.

Dad lifted Oliver up on his shoulders. Oliver felt a bit wobbly, but if he leant forward just a little, he could see right over the wet, leafy hedge. He could see the pond just below the hedge, in the damp, dark, misty garden. He felt very high up.

'Are you there, foggy frog?' called Oliver softly. There was no answer. Oliver leant over the hedge, trying to see if the frog was there.

'Come back!' said Oliver. 'I haven't said goodbye to you!'

But the frog had disappeared. It was either somewhere down in the long grass, or still under the hedge on its way to the pond.

'Come on Oliver,' said Dad, as Oliver wriggled about. 'You're heavy. Hurry up and post that letter.'

Oliver didn't reply, because all sorts of things suddenly happened very quickly. Oliver heard a soft little splash and a croak. The frog! He reached over further ... further ... to try and see the frog. Somehow he slipped and slithered – off Dad's shoulders and right over the hedge into the garden. He rolled down the bank towards the edge of the pond.

'Help!! Dad!!' screamed Oliver. He yelled and roared and shouted so loudly that he didn't hear Dad calling back to him, telling him he was just coming. He felt very frightened. Here he was all on his own, half in and half out of a pond in a strange garden in the fog. He was wet. His shoes and socks were muddy. His hands and knees were grassy and his hair and his clothes and his school-bag were covered in wet leaves and twigs. And the important letter lay floating on the weedy, muddy water.

'Dad!' yelled Oliver again. 'Dad! Where are you?'

Then he suddenly remembered about talking to God who was always there, wherever Oliver was. So he said to God: 'Hallo, God, it's Oliver. Please help me.'

'Now who's this?' said another voice, as Oliver crawled up the bank.

Oliver stared. It wasn't the frog, and it wasn't Dad. It was an elderly lady walking very slowly with a stick.

Oliver put his thumb in his mouth and stopped crying.

'I'm Oliver,' mumbled Oliver. 'I want my dad.'

'Up you get; he's coming,' said the lady. 'My name is Mrs Marshall. I'll go and open the gate. Then your dad can get in.'

Oliver didn't move. Dad came into the garden looking *very* angry.

'Oh OLIVER,' said Dad. 'What *are* you doing? Just look at you! You are always in trouble. Get up!' Dad hauled Oliver to his feet.

'Well this *is* a surprise,' said Mrs Marshall. 'I wondered whatever was happening in my garden! In you come and get dry. You *are* in a mess. In you come, please, both of you, for a minute.'

Before long Oliver was being washed and given a hot blackcurrant drink, and Dad was telephoning Mum to say why they'd be late home.

'I'm very glad to see you,' said Mrs Marshall, 'because my little cat, Sooty, hasn't come in this afternoon. I'm worried that he's got lost. And I can't walk very fast to look for him, and it's so dark and foggy. Would you be very kind and help me look for him before you go home?'

'I've got a cat called Zippy,' said Oliver. 'He's got stripes.'

It wasn't long before Dad and Oliver found Sooty. He'd climbed quite a long way up a tree and was crying to come down.

'I think it's my turn to go climbing this time,' said Dad to Oliver. 'You stand at the bottom of the tree and catch hold of Sooty, Oliver.'

Sooty was soon rescued, then Oliver remembered the important letter floating on the pond. Dad rescued that as well. Oliver looked for the frog, but it had gone. Then Oliver thought he heard a tiny croak.

'Goodbye, foggy frog,' said Oliver. 'You've caused me an awful lot of trouble, you know.'

But there was no answer, only a few bubbles on the surface of the water.

'We must dry the important letter before we post it,' said Dad. Then he said something to Mrs Marshall that Oliver didn't hear.

'Was it nice up the tree?' whispered Oliver in Sooty's furry ear.

'Yes, but it was foggy and lonely and I got frightened,' purred Sooty.

'So did I when I fell in the pond,' said Oliver.

Then they all said goodbye to each other.

'Thank you very much,' said Mrs Marshall. 'Do come again. I get lonely sometimes all on my own. It's been lovely having you to visit me.'

Then she said to Oliver: 'I've got my great-grandchildren coming next weekend. Would you like to come to tea?'

'Yes, please,' said Oliver. 'I would.'

Oliver made good friends with Frances who was six and Tom who was four. They ran all over Mrs Marshall's big house and made a lot of noise.

One day Oliver had another surprise. Some tickets came in an envelope.

'You remember that important letter, Oliver?' said Dad. 'That was a very special letter. It was for tickets for the pantomime for you and Polly and Vimal!! And Mrs Marshall said that Tom and Frances can come too.'

'Lots of surprises,' said Oliver. 'All because of a foggy frog!'

'Lots of surprises,' said Dad. 'All because God likes to make us happy.'

Oliver enjoyed every minute of the pantomime. He clapped and laughed and waved to the pantomime princess. In the interval, he said to God through a mouthful of choc-ice: 'This is fun, isn't it, God? Thank you for your nice surprises. And I'm glad you're always with me, wherever I am.'

Oliver and the star

It was nearly Christmas, and Oliver's school was getting ready for the Nativity play.

'We have to practise a lot,' grumbled Oliver to Mum and Dad. 'We keep having to do the same things over and over again. There's lots of FUSS.'

'You have to practise so that you get it right,' said Mum.

'All the best actors keep practising,' said Dad. 'It's called rehearsing.'

'I'm not a best actor,' said Oliver. 'I'm only a shepherd, and I have to carry a toy lamb. I'd rather carry teddy bear Bruin.'

'But Oliver,' said Mum, 'shepherds don't carry bears! They carry lambs. You are being difficult.'

Oliver was being difficult because he was very disappointed that he was a shepherd in the play. He had to sit by a pretend fire, and on the day of the play he was to wear his dressing-gown with a tea towel on his head, which seemed stupid. He didn't mind the rest; listening to the angels singing was all right, and dancing round the pretend fire was quite fun, except that Oliver just couldn't dance. The stars and the snowflakes and the

88

other shepherds all danced beautifully but Oliver couldn't get it right although he tried really, really hard.

'I keep tripping over other people,' sighed Oliver, 'and I keep falling over my own feet. They get in the way.'

What Oliver had really, really wanted was to be one of the wise men, because they were going to wear very grand cloaks, and carry beautiful shining gifts to Mary, who was his friend Anna. There was even gold material in the dressing up box, that nobody was wearing. And to make matters worse, Vimal was one of the wise men, who were kings. Jack was another and Harry another. He was the one in front who had to point at an imaginary star in the sky that led everyone to the baby Jesus while the other stars all danced.

If only I could have been a wise man, thought Oliver. Even his friend Scott had a rather special part because he wore an cow mask and had to say, 'Moo.'

Polly was an angel with a tinsel halo.

'Come along, children,' said Miss Harrison, 'you're supposed to look happy when you dance round the fire. Scott, you can't say "Moo" all the time like that. You're being silly. And Oliver – you're supposed to be dancing, not walking slowly. You're a shepherd, not a wise man.'

'I'm getting very, *very* tired of the play,' said Oliver to Mum. 'Miss Harrison keeps telling us about the baby Jesus and anyway, it's only a doll baby. It's all hidden in the straw.'

'It's only a doll baby in the play,' said Mum, 'but the real baby Jesus who was born long, long ago in a stable was the most special baby that has ever lived. He was God's own son who came to earth because God loves us all so much. But he didn't have a cot to sleep in. He slept in a manger where the animals feed.'

'If he was special, why was he put in a stable?' said Oliver.

'Because nobody knew who he was,' said Mum, 'except the shepherds, and the wise men, and his mother Mary, and Joseph of course.'

'The innkeeper wouldn't let them in,' said Oliver. 'In the play he says: "No Room!" when they come on a donkey, and sends them into the stable.'

Oliver thought he'd like to have a chat with that doll baby when nobody was looking. He'd tell it how he wanted to be a wise man instead of a shepherd.

When the wise men practised their parts, Harry, the wise man in the front, kept forgetting to point at the pretend star, and if he did remember, he dropped his gift. And because it was an imaginary star, the children found they were all pointing in different directions.

'This won't do at all,' said Miss Harrison, looking flustered. 'I think we must make a shiny star instead and put it up on the wall.'

Oliver was tired of rehearsing the play. He'd sat on the floor long enough. He shuffled around and fidgeted.

'Try and sit still, Oliver,' said Miss Harrison. 'BUT – you've just given me an idea. Come here a minute. You're the shepherd who's always walking nicely instead of dancing. Now, if we had a star on top of a long stick for someone to carry, that boy or girl could lead the way, while the other stars are doing their dance. And suppose that boy or girl is YOU, Oliver?'

Oliver felt very excited. Then he looked worried.

'But I'm a shepherd,' said Oliver, 'so how can I

be a star?'

'Well, I think perhaps we have enough shepherds,' said Miss Harrison. 'So how would you like to hold the big star - and BE the star – instead? There's some lovely tinselly gold material in the dressing-up box that you can wear. And we'll make a big gold star on a gold stick for you to carry and lead the way. You'll be showing the wise men and everyone the way to the baby Jesus. You'll be very special!'

Oliver felt very, very pleased and happy. A star!

'I'm not a shepherd any more,' said Oliver to Mum. 'I'm a star!'

He practised carrying the star at school and at home.

'Whatever are you doing?' asked Mr Jolly when he saw Oliver walking slowly and carefully up and down the garden path holding up a stick.

'I'm a star,' said Oliver. 'I'm very special, you know.'

'Well fancy that, Oliver,' said Mr Jolly. 'I always knew you were very special – but a star! Fancy that!'

When the day of the play came, Oliver nearly felt shy, when everyone was all dressed up and he saw the rows of mums and dads. But he did enjoy being dressed in gold material and carrying the star. He led the wise men from behind the audience, all the way to the manger.

'I'm showing everyone where baby Jesus is,' thought Oliver proudly.

All the children had to gather round the baby Jesus at the end of the play. They sang 'Happy Birthday, Dear Jesus'.

Oliver liked that. But he had to stand at the edge of the group with the star, so he couldn't get too close to

the doll baby. He still hadn't chatted to it, which was a pity. Then, suddenly, he didn't want to, anyway, because he knew that there was always the real Jesus he could talk to and would answer him, baby Jesus who had been born in a stable long, long ago. He was God's own son; God the great God who had made the world and who liked Oliver very much. That's why there was all the fuss at Christmas!

'I'm glad it's Christmas,' whispered Oliver inside himself to the real Jesus. 'And I'm glad there was a star, and I'm glad you were born. If I'd been the innkeeper I'd have let you come in.'

Then Oliver felt so very happy that he gave the audience a very big surprise. He DANCED! Everyone laughed and clapped Oliver loudly. Mum and Dad and Sally and Dave clapped loudest of all. Oliver bowed.

'Oh OLIVER,' said Miss Harrison, 'I thought you couldn't dance!'

'I can now because I'm a star,' said Oliver. 'I'm dancing for baby Jesus.'

Other stories suitable for reading aloud to under 6s:

Little Ted Lost
Mary Howard

At half-past seven it was time for bed. After he'd had his bath, put on his Fireman Sam pyjamas and cleaned his teeth, Simon dashed into his bedroom and jumped on the bed. He looked under his duvet and under his pillow but his teddy wasn't there. 'Where is he, Granny? Where's my Little Ted?'

A collection of short stories and poems about Simon, his family, friends and Little Ted. Simon is four at the beginning of the book, but becomes five and starts school during the time covered by the stories.

Zac and the Multi-coloured Spidajig
Kathleen Crawford

'Yummy!' thought Sophie, 'they look delicious.'
    She was just opening her mouth and putting out her tongue to eat the first strawberry when it happened.
    'HIC,' went Sophie, and she shot high into the air, completely missing the strawberry she wanted to eat.

Meet Sophie, the frog with hiccups, Zac and his

monster spider called Spidajig and Mrs McMuddle, who goes to buy a loaf of tomato soup.

A book of lively short stories, poems and simple prayers.

The Castle
Ro Willoughby

'Dad,' Ben said. 'I've been thinking. Do you know what I would like?'

'Can I guess?' his father answered.

Ben waited.

His dad smiled and then chuckled.

'You'd like me to make you a castle when we get home, wouldn't you?'

When Dad builds a castle for Ben and Becky they make new friends like Chippy and Mrs Weetabix and they have fun helping Dad.

Pancake Fingers
Ro Willoughby

Mum brought in the funny-shaped pancake. It looked more like an octopus with a round bit in the middle and several fingers stretching out from the centre.

'How shall I roll this?' Becky asked.

Then she jumped off her stool with a whoop of laughter and ran round to Ben.

'Do you know what this pancake looks like?' she asked.

'No,' Ben and Jo said together.

'A spider,' she shouted.

'Creepy crawly, here I come
Creepy, creepy crawly.'

Ben and Becky often ask questions like, 'Why does skin get wet and sticky when we get hot?' 'Why do we have toes?' They also enjoy singing rhymes and having fun with friends.

More entertaining stories about Ben and Becky.

All these titles are also available as story cassettes.